The Bridesmaid Wears Track Shoes

The Bridesmaid Wears Track Shoes

Marilyn D. Anderson

*Cover photo by Bichsel Morris
Photographic Illustrators.*

Published by Willowisp Press, Inc.
401 E. Wilson Bridge Road, Worthington, Ohio 43085

Printed in the United States of America
10 9 8 7 6 5 4 3 2

ISBN 0-87406-008-7

To Milo and Hazel Swanson,
with all my love.

One

I guess it's no wonder my family keeps trying to forget I exist. The other kids all have naturally curly hair, perfect skin and talent. There's my older sister, Cheryl, who's a senior at the local college, Jason, the starting forward on our high school basketball team, Jeremy, the brain of the freshman class, and my baby sister Brenda. I'm just plain old Roxie Wood, sort of a brand-X kind of fourteen year old.

This whole thing with Cheryl and her boyfriend, Matt, came up about two months ago. The five of us and my mom and stepfather were sitting around the supper table. As usual, my mind was on my first basketball practice of the season. I had made more free throws than anyone else on the team, and I was dying to tell everyone about it. But, before I got started, Cheryl took over the conversation.

"None for me," she said, pushing away the bowl of macaroni and cheese as if it was poison. "Matthew likes his girls willowy, so I'll just have a salad and a couple crackers."

Mom's new husband, Roger, picked right up on that. "Matthew? Who's Matthew, and whatever happened to good old Larry Volkswagen?" he asked.

Jason snorted. "She probably got tired of watching that guy eat. What a pig!" he said.

Cheryl shot him a look guaranteed to frost your pumpkin. "The name is Heerwagon, for your information, and Larry is just too juvenile for any lasting relationship."

"So this Matthew is more mature?" my mom asked skeptically.

"Oh, yes," my sister assured her. "Matthew has his future all planned out. He's going to be a professional basketball coach."

"That's nice," said Mom. "Do tell us more about him, his last name for instance. Is he from Richfield?"

"No, he's originally from New Albany. His family moved here about the time I started college," she said.

"And what did you say his last name is?" Mom persisted.

"Block. His name is Matthew Block," Cheryl said.

"Not THE Matt Block?" Jason demanded suddenly. "The star center of last year's Wildcat team?" he asked.

Cheryl nodded. "He's the cutest guy on the team, too."

Jason grabbed one of the earphones to Jeremy's ever-present cassette headset and yelled at him. "Cheryl's going with Matt Block!" But Jeremy only grabbed his earphone back and slouched deeper in his chair.

I tried to change the subject. "I may be the best free-throw shooter on our team this year," I said brightly. But no one seemed to hear me.

"How did you and Matt get together?" Jason asked.

"Who cares?" I said to myself.

"Oh, it was so romantic," Cheryl gushed. "Larry had just managed to get that ratty old Ford of his stuck in the mud, and Matthew came along to rescue us."

"Where had you and Larry gone to get stuck in the mud?" Mom asked curiously. "It hasn't rained in weeks."

Cheryl squirmed a little at that, and Jason giggled. "Oh, we sort of got lost on the way home from a party," she said lamely.

"Mom, may I have a gerbil?" Brenda cut in.

"We don't need any pets around here right now," said Mom. "The contractors are coming to remodel the kitchen any day."

"But you said they'd be here before school started," Brenda reminded her.

"They are supposed to come as soon as possible," Mom explained. "It's just taking them a little longer than we thought it would."

Soon everyone was talking about the dumb plans for the kitchen, and I gave up hope of getting into the conversation. I bet Dad would have listened to me if he'd been here.

I don't know if Cheryl talked more about Matt during the next few weeks because I tuned her out. Our first basketball game was coming up, and I had to get in shape. One night Jason caught me eating too much.

"Hey, leave some meatloaf for the rest of us," he complained as I took a third slice.

"I'm trying to eat plenty of protein so I'll be ready for Tuesday night," I told him.

"What's Tuesday night?" Mom asked.

"My first basketball game of the season," I said too loudly. How could she have forgotten? I wondered.

She frowned. "Oh, Roxie, I'm sorry. I can't be there. I have a committee meeting that night."

"Never mind," I told her. "I'm sure Dad will come."

Jason snickered. "Dad? Come to a girls' basketball game? He told me once he'd rather watch wallpaper peel."

I made a face at him and looked down at my plate. I planned to call Dad anyway because

Jason doesn't know everything.

I waited until the kitchen was empty to make the call. It felt weird to be calling Dad because we hardly saw him anymore. I even practiced what I would say.

The phone rang a bunch of times before anyone answered it. Then a little kid's voice said, "Hi, Grandma."

Grandma? No one ever called me that before. "Hello, is this the Norman Wood residence?" I asked.

"I'm Thor," said the voice.

"Thor who?" I asked.

"Thor Ramone Wood. Where's Grandpa?" he asked.

"Grandpa isn't here. May I please speak to your father?" I asked.

"Where's Grandpa?" the voice insisted.

"Thanks anyway," I said as I hung up.

It turned out that I didn't get to play much in the game against Northside. I was miserable sitting on the bench watching our team get creamed. It was a good thing Dad didn't come. With only two minutes left on the clock, the coach finally put in my best friend Heidi and me. She probably figured with the score 35 to 10 it couldn't hurt. One of the Northside girls was shooting a free throw so I took my place under the basket next to the "seven footer" I was supposed to guard. The Northside girl put the ball in the air, but it was short. It bounced off the rim and landed right in my hands. Without even thinking I fired it toward Heidi, she passed to Gretchen and we had two points.

I went after the ball like a tiger in the closing seconds only to hear the ref's whistle. I'd committed a foul, and the Northside girl sank both free throws to make the final score 37 to 12.

Heidi and I went slinking off the floor with our arms around each other. "Wish we'd been put in sooner," she said dejectedly.

"Yeah," I agreed. "But it probably wouldn't have helped much."

Our locker room was deathly quiet as we listened to Northside celebrate next door. How could they have beaten us so badly? I wondered. If the whole season was going to be like this, we might as well give up right now.

"Don't let this shake you too much," our coach said. "Northside is always tough. You'll do better against Higbee."

I wanted to believe her, but things looked pretty black. Heidi and I were feeling so low that we almost ran into Cheryl as we came out of the locker room door.

"What are you doing here?" I gasped.

She shrugged. "It seemed as if someone from

the family ought to come. Besides, I thought Dad might be here," she said.

"I never got to ask him," I said, shoving my hands into my pockets.

"Too bad," she answered glumly, and the three of us headed home in silence. If she had made one smart remark, I'd have slugged her, but she didn't.

Two

I remember Cheryl talking about Matt again one Saturday morning a few weeks later. We were having pancakes, and the boys were inhaling theirs as usual. Since my sister had just been to Matt's house for the first time, she was telling Mom about it.

"Their house is like a palace," Cheryl said eagerly. "They have two huge fireplaces, a sunken living room, a pool, a sauna, a rec room with all kinds of video games . . ."

"What kind of business is Mr. Block in?" Mom asked.

"Hauling garbage. The company's name is Destinkly Yours," Cheryl said.

We all groaned and Cheryl continued. "You should see all the bowling trophies Mr. Block has, and Matt's mother looks like Dolly Parton.

"Say, I'd like to meet her," said Roger, suddenly coming out of his early-morning fog.

By now Jeremy had finished stuffing his face. He pulled off his headset long enough to ask,

"Hey, Mom, can I have an advance on my allowance?"

"You've already spent your allowance for the next two months," Mom reminded him. So he shrugged, put his headset back in place and boogied out the door.

"I have a karate class at ten o'clock," Jason announced. "Can I use the car?"

"Mom, my birthday is this week, and I want a gerbil," Brenda insisted.

My mother shook her head. "Jason, I'm going shopping this afternoon so that car better be back by noon. Brenda, we'll talk about your gerbil this afternoon if you leave me alone this morning. I have lots of work to do around here."

That was my cue to beat it unless I wanted to get stuck cleaning my room or worse. I went over to Heidi's, but she was babysitting her little brother. We ended up playing Monopoly while we watched T.V.

I got home pretty late that afternoon to find a surprise in our kitchen. Robert Redford's double was standing there holding a little brown gerbil up to his face with Brenda and Cheryl looking on.

"Roxie, look. Mom bought me a gerbil," Brenda said excitedly. "I'm going to call him Homer."

"Oh, yeah?" I mumbled. Now I admit Homer

was cute, but our visitor seemed to be over-doing it a bit. I never saw a guy his age talking to an animal like that.

"Matthew, this is my sister, Roxie," said Cheryl. "She's going out for both basketball and track this year."

Matt turned his sleepy blue eyes on me, and I could see they just matched his sweater. Now why couldn't I have had dimples and wavy blond hair like that? I wondered.

"Hi, there," he said with a grin that made me try to hide my braces.

"Hi," I mumbled stupidly.

"How's your team doing this year?" he asked, although his attention was really on Homer.

"Uh, we've only had one game so far," I said.

"Oh, it's too early to tell, eh?" he said as he tickled the gerbil's ear. "What's your event in track?"

"The hurdles," I said.

"Guess what," Brenda interrupted. "Matt had a hamster when he was little, and he has a wheel at home he said I could have."

"I had a bunch of hamsters," he explained. "They were always having babies."

"Oh, look at you," Cheryl said suddenly. "You're getting hair all over your sweater, and it's almost time to leave."

17

He looked down and handed Homer back to Brenda. "It's not too bad," he said, picking off a few of the hairs.

While Brenda put the gerbil down on the floor to investigate, Cheryl and Matt picked away at the sweater. Then Cheryl had an idea. She bustled over to get a roll of plastic tape and made a big wad of it. "This ought to take it off," she said, and she started rubbing at the hairs.

As she used up each wad, she added it to the ball she was forming on the counter. When the ball had grown to the size of a baseball, it suddenly fell and landed right on poor Homer. He gave a little squeal and headed for the living room with all of us grabbing at him.

Just as Matt started through the kitchen door, Mom was coming in. They bumped into each other. "Hi, I'm Matt Block," he said, blushing slightly.

"May I ask what's going on?" Mom asked.

Brenda was bawling at the top of her lungs so it wasn't easy to explain. Finally Mom sputtered, "Oh, my goodness!" Then Mom headed for the living room yelling, "We've got to catch that animal. I don't want a dirty rat running all over the house."

"He's not a rat, and gerbils are very clean," Matt said quickly as he followed her. "But we'd better catch him before he gets hurt."

All five of us were crawling around on our hands and knees when Matt spotted a mass of tape stuck to one of the drapes. He picked up poor Homer and started back toward the kitchen as he talked soothingly to the gerbil.

"Hey, what are you going to do?" Mom demanded as he reached the sink.

"Well, we have to get the tape off of him. I figured I'd get it wet," he explained.

"Not in MY kitchen," Mom said angrily. "You'll have to take him in the bathroom."

"No, someone else can do that job," Cheryl said firmly. "We're going to be late for the party if we don't get going right now."

"Gosh, I can't leave Homer in a fix like this," Matt objected.

"Roxie can handle things, can't you, Roxie?" asked my dear sister.

I shrugged. "I suppose so," I said, taking the sticky mess from Matt. I'm not sure who suffered more, me or Homer, but I finally managed to get him back to normal.

* * * * *

When I got home the next night from our game against Higbee, I felt great. We beat them by 11 points, and I made two of them. Since there was no one in the kitchen, I thought I might tell Dad about it. Grabbing a couple of cookies, I dialed the number.

"Hello, Grandma?" said a voice I recognized immediately.

"Listen kid, I'm not your grandma," I said fiercely. "Now go get your father because I want to talk to him."

"Don't want to," said the voice, and he hung up, the turkey.

I was in my room doing homework at about 9:30 when I heard voices in the living room. One of them sounded like Cheryl's. Gee, she's home awfully early, I thought.

The voices went on a while and then they began to get louder. I heard Mom say, "I don't care. You're too young to get married!"

I let my pencil fall. "Married? Cheryl's getting married?" I gasped.

Three

I had to hear more, so being careful not to wake Brenda who shares my room, I slipped out the door and closed it behind me. "But Mom, I'm 21 years old," Cheryl was saying. "That's old enough to get married."

Holy cow! My sister wants to get married, I thought as I plopped down on the top step of the stairway. She must be crazy.

"I don't care," said Mom. "We've all struggled to see that you get a college education. Now that you're ready to graduate, you want to throw it all away."

"What's wrong with getting married?" Cheryl asked.

"Nothing," Mom said. "When you've had a taste of being on your own, and when you've proved a few things to yourself, I'll be delighted to see you get married."

"But Matthew is going off to grad school June fifteenth. We want to get married so that I can go with him," Cheryl said.

I heard Mom give sort of a bitter laugh. "If you do, you'll regret it. You'll be making the same mistake I did. Believe me. You'll always be looking for a better job, trying to make ends meet."

"Mom!" Cheryl protested. "We're in love. Can't you understand that?"

"So you're in love. See each other on weekends. Why, he doesn't even have a job. How can he support you?" Mom asked.

"He's going to find a job and so am I," Cheryl said firmly.

Talk her out of it Mom, I thought desperately.

"Cheryl, don't be silly," said Mom. "Don't rush into something as important as marriage. You need time to think about it."

"Mother, my mind is made up. You can't stop me," Cheryl said.

"Well, don't expect me to pay for a big fancy wedding then," Mom snapped.

"All right, I won't," Cheryl retorted, heading my way. "Good night, Mother."

I ducked around the corner and tried to think. I had to talk to my sister, but what would I say? She headed for the bathroom, and by the time she came out, I was ready for her. "Cheryl," I called softly, "I want to talk to you. Please."

She gave a little jump and looked around

nervously. "Roxie," she hissed. "What do you want?"

"I know all about you and Matt," I said earnestly. "You can't get married. You just can't."

She turned on the light to her room and drew me inside. "What do you mean by that?" she demanded.

"You don't want to start cooking and cleaning full time, do you?" I asked desperately. "You were going to be a teacher."

She relaxed then and began to laugh. "Roxie, teachers can be married, you know," she said.

I hadn't thought of that. "But you can't leave us," I persisted. "I'd have to do all the dishes by myself, and the boys won't have anyone to pick on but me."

"The boys aren't that bad," she said more gently. "And Brenda is big enough to help you with dishes. Now what's really bothering you?"

I sniffed and thought a minute. "Maybe I just don't want things to change around here anymore," I admitted. "It's bad enough since Dad moved out."

"Oh, so that's it," Cheryl said. "You think I'm breaking up the family still more. Well I guess I am, but it can't be helped. I have my own life to live. You can see that, can't you?"

"I guess so," I answered half-heartedly.

"Of course you can," she said, trying hard to sound cheerful. "Why, look at it this way, you'll be able to have your own room if I leave. That's something you've always wanted."

"I don't want that anymore," I muttered. But she was nudging me gently toward the door so I left. I went to the bathroom to stare at myself in the mirror. Would I ever want to get married? I wondered. Not likely. I just couldn't understand why Cheryl was so eager to get tied down.

When the boys heard about Cheryl's wedding plans at breakfast, they could hardly believe it. "Are you kidding?" jeered Jason. "You're a rotten cook, and you'd make a terrible wife."

Jeremy, who happened to be changing tapes, agreed. "The only thing you can cook is pizza. Matt must be sick in the head to consider marrying you."

Brenda, however, thought it was a great idea. "Oh, boy, can I be the flower girl?" she asked eagerly. "I want to throw flowers all over the place."

"Yes, Honey," Cheryl assured her. "I'm counting on you to be the flower girl."

"Whoa there, wait just a minute," cried Mom. "I haven't agreed to any wedding. I still say you're too young."

"Your mother is right, Cheryl," Roger said, looking up from the newspaper.

"And I say we're going to get married no matter what you two think," Cheryl countered.

"Who's going to pay for it?" Mom asked.

"Dad will," Cheryl said confidently.

"Ha," said Mom. "He won't go for the idea either."

"We won't know that for sure until we ask him, will we?" Cheryl shot back.

"Right," Mom agreed. "And the sooner you ask him the better. How about today?"

"Matthew and I have plans to look at engagement rings," Cheryl sputtered. She was beginning to sound a lot less sure of herself.

"I think we need to discuss this with your father," said Mom. "I'm calling him right now."

"Tell him I want to see him, too," I called after her, but she didn't answer.

When Mom returned she was grinning from ear to ear. "It's all set," she announced triumphantly. "I told him Cheryl has some big news for him, and he's invited you all over for supper tonight."

"Who said I wanted to go?" Jason objected. "Mike and I were going to the movies."

"That's too bad," said Mom. "It's time you met your father's new family."

Cheryl and I looked at each other. This was going to be *some* evening.

Four

DAD and his new wife lived in one of Richfield's most remote suburbs. We all had plenty of time to think on the way. Only Brenda had been allowed to stay home when she told Mom, "I don't like your old husband." The rest of us didn't know what to expect. Jeremy looked lost without his headset, and I couldn't help wondering what Thor would be like in person. We'd heard that Dad's new wife was super smart. She worked as a child psychologist even though she had two little boys.

Roger left us at the end of Dad's sidewalk. That left Cheryl, Jason, Jeremy, and me staring at the impressive ranch-style house ahead and trying to work up the courage to go inside. Finally Jason said, "I'm hungry. Come on." He walked up the steps and rang the doorbell.

There was a sound of running feet. Then a dark-haired boy with huge brown eyes looked out the door. "We don't want any," he cried, slamming the door in our faces. That had to be Thor.

Frowning, Jason leaned on the bell again only to have the same little boy return with a smaller version of himself. They were both naked! For a moment they studied us and we stared at them. Then they both stuck their tongues out at us and slammed the door.

The third time Jason was too fast for them. He stuck his foot in the door before they could slam it and bellowed, "Dad, are you in here?"

Realizing their little game was over, Thor promptly kicked Jason in the knee and turned to run. Jason grunted with pain as Dad hurried to grab the culprit.

"Thor," Dad said firmly. "Was that a wise thing to do? You won't have many friends if you treat them like that."

"Don't want these friends," the boy announced and stomped off.

"Go away," the smaller boy yelled and followed his brother.

"You'll have to forgive them," Dad said with an embarrassed laugh. "They're going through a very difficult phase right now."

The four of us looked at each other in shock. Difficult phase? Those kids were monsters. Why didn't he flatten them? I wondered.

Dad led us through the living room. "Come this way," he directed. "I want you to meet Rachel."

Judging by all the new and expensive things I saw, I decided that Dad must really be making money these days. Rachel was quite a surprise, too. She didn't look much older than Cheryl and she was quite beautiful. Her trim shirtwaist dress made her look like one of those housewives you see on soap operas. She had something cooking in one of those hollow dome things called a "wok." I couldn't tell what it was.

"Children, this is Rachel," my father said proudly.

"Welcome," she answered in a musical voice. "We're so glad you could come."

"Pleased to meet you," we murmured.

"Now I want to show you my greenhouse," Dad said eagerly. "It's just off the family room."

Just then something small and hard hit me on the cheek.

"Thor," Rachel said mildly, "if you can't behave more appropriately, you will have to go to your room."

My cheek hurt. "Just let me at that little creep," I said to myself.

Dad looked uncomfortable and hustled us out saying, "The greenhouse is this way."

The small plastic building was attached to the south side of the house, and there was barely room for two people inside. Dad stayed outside with Cheryl and me while the boys went in. I was really glad to have Dad with us to guard against further attacks from the rear.

"The vegetables are mine and the herbs are Rachel's," he explained, pointing through the plastic. "Organically grown food is much healthier than anything you can buy in a store, and it tastes better, too."

When it was Cheryl's and my turn to go inside the greenhouse, I promptly started sneezing. I didn't like Rachel's herbs, I didn't like her kids, and I decided I wasn't too keen on Rachel herself.

We all went into the family room after that and settled ourselves in the plush new furniture as best we could. For several minutes no one spoke. When it started getting embarrassing, Dad asked stiffly, "Well, how are things at school?"

"Fine," we all agreed.

"Are you keeping up your grades?"

We all nodded.

"How's the ball team doing, Jason?"

"Good," Jason assured him.

"I think about you kids often, but things have been so busy at the lab," he said uneasily.

You're not too busy for Rachel and those brats of hers, I wanted to say.

Dad smiled and tried again. "Cheryl, your mother said you have some big news for me. I'd like to hear it," he said.

She squirmed uncomfortably. She was about to say something when Rachel appeared to announce that dinner was ready. I got to my feet quickly, feeling guilty for the relief I felt. We filed into the dining room and seated ourselves. The table was set with crystal glassware, cloth napkins and fresh flowers. The two little boys appeared and sat on either side of Dad. At least they were fully clothed now.

Rachel set bowls of brown rice, stir-fried vegetables and some kind of seafood salad on the table. The rice stuff looked sort of gross, and I wasn't too excited about the rest of it either. But I took a small helping of everything and began to eat. Thor and his brother weren't so polite.

"Don't want any," said Thor, shaking his head.

"Don't want any," said his echo.

"Then what would you like for dinner?" Rachel asked gently.

"Cornflakes," Thor stated flatly.

"Cornflakes," came the echo. So Rachel went to get some cornflakes.

Maybe they aren't so dumb, I thought, sampling the rice warily. Yuk! I tried mixing it with the vegetables, but nothing helped.

After dinner Rachel took the boys off to read

them a story. The rest of us found ourselves back in the family room. Cheryl and I sat on the couch while the boys sat on the floor.

"Well, Cheryl," Dad prodded, "I've been trying to guess what your big news might be. You didn't land a teaching job already, did you?" he asked.

She blushed. "No, that's not it."

"Then what is it?" he urged. "Tell me."

"I'm getting married," she answered softly.

"Married?" he repeated. "This is rather sudden, isn't it?"

"I told her she was crazy," said Jason.

"She can't even cook," Jeremy added.

"Talk her out of it," I begged.

"Matthew and I have been going together for about three months," Cheryl explained. "We're in love, and we want to be together always."

Dad looked at her and shook his head. "Of course you're in love," he said almost bitterly. "I fell in and out of love once a week at your age, but marriage is a big step."

"I know that," Cheryl retorted. "I am an adult now, you know."

Dad rubbed his neck thoughtfully. "Well," he said at last, "if you're sure this marriage is right for you, then I say go ahead with it."

I wanted to scream, "Dad, you're supposed to talk her out of it." But I didn't.

Five

CHERYL'S eyes shone. "You mean you approve of me getting married?" she asked.

He shrugged. "Why not? You'd probably go ahead with it anyway." Then he turned to say something to Jason, and I gave Cheryl a nudge.

"You didn't tell him he has to pay for the wedding," I reminded her. Surely that would make Dad change his mind.

"Give me a chance," she hissed back.

Dad noticed us whispering and said, "Is there something else I should know?"

"Well, yes," Cheryl admitted. "Mom says she won't pay for the wedding. Will you?"

Dad snorted. "I should have guessed. Knowing your mother the way I do, I should have guessed. Well, how big an affair are we talking about?" he asked.

"Oh, nothing too huge," my sister said eagerly. "Just some friends and relatives."

"What kind of wedding things will you need?" Dad asked.

"Only a dress, some flowers and a little food," Cheryl said.

"That's all? Why, of course I'll pay for it. Hey, Rachel, come here," he called.

"Thanks, Dad," Cheryl cried. "I knew I could count on you."

Then Rachel appeared at the door with her two little boys in tow. "What's up?" she asked pleasantly.

"Cheryl is getting married," Dad said. "I thought you could help her with the wedding plans, and I know she'll want you to play the cello at the ceremony."

"That's wonderful," Rachel answered enthusiastically. "I love weddings. Have you decided on a place yet, Cheryl? Garden ceremonies are terribly popular these days."

"Well, uh, no," Cheryl admitted.

"Then come with me," said Rachel, steering my sister out the door. "I was the maid of honor in a garden wedding last year, and I want you to see the gorgeous photographs."

When Rachel left, Thor and his brother went over and jumped on my father. "Give us a horseback ride," Thor demanded.

"Horsey, horsey," cried his brother.

Dad shook his head. "Not now, boys. I have company."

"We want to play horsey," Thor insisted, and

he punched my father as hard as he could.

I thought that Dad would surely defend himself. I could see that in his eyes he wanted to, but instead he got down on all fours and let the boys jump on him. "It's just a phase they're going through," he assured us.

When Dad dropped us off that night, Mom was waiting. "Well, what did your father have to say about the wedding?" she demanded.

Cheryl gave her a smug look. "He said he'd pay for the whole thing," she said.

"He did?" gasped Mom. "Didn't he even try to talk you out of it?"

My sister shook her head. "Nope, he wants me to be happy." And she headed up the stairs without looking back.

Mom was silent for a minute. Then she asked half-heartedly, "How was supper?"

"Weird," said Jason.

"Boring," Jeremy added.

"Yuk," I agreed.

It took me a long time to go to sleep that night. I couldn't stop thinking about how Dad had let me down. He never even tried to stop Cheryl, and he hadn't talked to me at all.

Mom was in a state of shock the whole next day. She fidgeted during church, and she made Roger take us out for dinner. As soon as we got home, she called Dad. The kitchen door was closed so all I could hear was a phrase now and then. "She's too young," and "What about a career?" came through distinctly. Later that day I learned that Mom had let me down, too.

"There's going to be a wedding this spring," she informed us. "So we'd all better get used to the idea."

We had Monday off for President's Day, but the day was cold and rainy. I called Heidi, and she said she'd come over. We took a bag of potato chips up to my room and settled down on the bed to eat them.

"What's new?" she asked casually.

"Not much," I lied.

"Are we going to do something or just eat?" she asked.

"I don't know," I muttered.

"We could listen to some records," she suggested.

"I don't feel like it," I said.

"Want to play a game or put together a puzzle?" she asked.

"Naw," I mumbled.

"I could comb your hair," she suggested.

"Okay," I agreed, finding my comb and sitting up straight on the bed. After she'd combed for a while, I said, "I may be getting a room of my own pretty soon."

Heidi stopped combing. "Oh, yeah? How

come?" she wondered.

"Cheryl's getting married," I said as evenly as I could.

Heidi clapped her hands and bounced around. "Really?" she asked excitedly. "Are you going to be in it?"

"I don't know," I said.

She came over and gave me a little push on the shoulder. "Oh, Roxie, of course, you are! I've always wanted to be a bridesmaid. Just think of the fancy dress you'll get to wear and all the flowers!"

I didn't say anything.

"Well, aren't you excited?" she demanded.

"No," I told her. "If Cheryl leaves things won't be the same."

"Of course they won't," she said lightly. "What's her fiancé like?"

"He's okay," I admitted.

"Is he cute?" she asked.

"Yeah," I said, blushing. "Real cute."

"Oh, I want to meet him. Maybe he has a brother," Heidi cooed.

I gave her a grin. "Nope. Just two sisters. Sorry," I said.

"Did he buy her a ring?" she asked, eagerly.

"Not yet. They went window shopping today," I mumbled.

"How exciting," Heidi cried, dancing around

my room again.

By then the potato chips were gone. A delicious smell was coming from the kitchen and it made us want to investigate. We found Cheryl and Matt drinking cocoa while they watched Mom frost a cake. I could see by Heidi's expression that she approved of Matt. She was practically drooling.

"We saw a ring at Groth's that's just perfect," Cheryl was telling my mother. "It has a huge diamond in the center and a bunch of smaller ones around that."

"Sounds expensive," Mom said skeptically.

"Well, it is, sort of," Cheryl admitted. "But dear, sweet Matthew said he wants me to have the best, didn't you, Honey?"

"Uh, huh," Matt grunted, never taking his eyes off the cake.

Then Mom noticed Heidi and me. "Roxie, please introduce Matthew to your friend," she directed.

"Matt, this is Heidi," I said, hiding my braces as best I could.

"Hi," he said, flashing a mouthful of perfect teeth.

Gosh, but he was gorgeous, I thought again.

"Hi," Heidi answered shyly.

Then Cheryl began to tug at his arm. "Honey," she insisted. "We've got to make some important decisions today like who's going to be in the wedding."

He glanced at her for a moment before his eyes went to the cake again. "Yeah, I suppose so," he mumbled.

"We'll have Roxie and my brothers, and Brenda will be the flower girl."

"Sure," he agreed. "And my sisters."

Cheryl frowned. "But I want to ask Nancy, Lisa, Sybil, and Laurie. That makes seven girls," she said.

"So?" he answered, reaching for the cake Mom was offering him.

Good grief, I thought, there won't be anyone left in the audience.

"The church is rather small for that many bridesmaids," my mother observed.

Cheryl looked thoughtful. "Well, I'm not sure we're having it in the church," she said.

"What do you mean by that?" Mom demanded. "Where else would you have it?"

"Rachel seems to think a garden wedding would be nice," Cheryl said.

"Whose garden, and what if it rains?" Mom protested.

Just then Brenda walked in with Homer. "Matt, look," she squealed. "Homer likes popcorn."

"Well, sure," he said, finishing his cake

quickly. "Gerbils like all kinds of different foods. Does he like the wheel I brought him?"

"Oh, just come and see," Brenda begged.

As he started after her, Cheryl said crossly, "Matthew, we need to discuss the wedding. Do you want a church ceremony or not?"

"You decide," he said lightly and followed Brenda.

"He seems as enthusiastic about this wedding as I am," I mumbled.

Six

"MEN," fumed Cheryl.

"Matthew certainly seems to like animals," Heidi observed.

"Too bad he can't get as interested in our wedding plans," muttered my sister.

"Typical, very typical," Mom informed us. "Matt probably won't object to anything you decide about the ceremony, but you'd better consult his mother."

"His mother?" asked Cheryl, wrinkling up her nose. "What's his mother have to do with this?"

"You'll be seeing a lot of Matt's family from now on," Mom explained. "Their opinion of your plans could be important for years to come."

Cheryl thought about that for a moment and sighed. "I guess you have a point there," she agreed. "I'll have a talk with Mrs. Block soon."

* * * * *

The basketball season was ending now, and our team's record wasn't too hot. I could hardly wait for track season to start because I knew I could help that team. But our first track practice was on Friday, and Friday was a crummy day. Heidi went home with the flu, Mom had to work overtime, and Homer fell down the laundry chute. Everyone was too busy looking for that silly gerbil to want to hear about my chances to win the conference title in the hurdles.

I was doing dishes the next morning when Cheryl finally came down. As she made herself some toast, she kept shoving her new diamond ring under my nose. Finally I muttered, "So poor old Matt came through. Did he have to hock his car to swing it?"

Cheryl looked a little hurt and snapped, "No. If you must know, this ring is much cheaper than the one I had picked out."

"Let me see," said Jason, appearing from nowhere. When Cheryl held her ring out for him to admire, he asked with a grin, "Can I borrow it some time?"

She looked at him curiously. "What on earth for?" she asked.

"I hear that diamonds do a neat job of cutting glass, and I thought . . . " Jason started.

Cheryl gave a little squeal and yanked her hand back. "Get away from me," she cried.

Rachel called after breakfast. She had just heard that weddings were sometimes held in the rose garden of our city park. She thought Cheryl ought to consider that possibility.

"But how would I keep away joggers and kids playing baseball?" Cheryl asked.

Rachel hadn't thought of that.

* * * * *

Mom, Cheryl, and I went into the city that afternoon. We were supposed to be looking for kitchen cabinets. However, a fabulous dress in one of the store windows caught my sister's eye. She had to try it on, and finally Mom agreed to go with her.

The store's bridal department was way up on the fourth floor, and was it fancy! A woman with bleached hair and gobs of jewelry seemed to be in charge. She looked about as friendly as poison ivy until she spotted Cheryl's diamond. Then her attitude changed a lot.

"May I help you, dear?" she asked in an icy voice.

"Yes," my sister told her. "I'd like to try on the wedding dress you have in the window."

"Certainly, dear," gushed the woman. "What size, please?"

"A ten," Cheryl said.

The saleswoman nodded and almost bowed in her eagerness to please Cheryl. "This way to the fitting room, please," she said.

We followed her through velvet curtains into an elegant room dominated by three huge gold-framed mirrors. The walls around the mirrors were papered in beige satin with flowers and tiny bells on them. Against the walls stood several antique chairs. Everything looked so nice that I wished I were a princess.

The woman disappeared and returned seconds later to hang a mass of white lace next to one of the mirrors. "Here you are, dear," she oozed. "Be sure to call me when you're ready."

Cheryl was too impressed by the dress to do anything but stare at it for a moment. Even I had to admit it was awesome. There were so many layers of material and so many pearl buttons that I wouldn't have known how to put it on.

Then, as Cheryl began to slip out of her jeans, Mom sprang into action. Wiping her hands on her own brown slacks, Mom undid the little buttons. Together, she and Cheryl managed to get the dress over Cheryl's head and button up the back. Suddenly we saw before us, not my sister, but someone out of a fairy tale. She was beautiful.

"You should have worn panty hose and a slip for this," said Mom, wiping something from her eye. "Those green socks with the orange checks look a little out of place."

Cheryl nodded without taking her eyes off the image in the mirror.

"May I come in?" asked the saleswoman, peeking through the curtains.

"Uh huh," Cheryl answered. She seemed hypnotized by her own reflection.

"Oh, my," gushed the saleswoman in a near swoon. "How lovely you look. That dress was made for you."

"I really like it," Cheryl agreed breathlessly.

"The perfect dress for a once-in-a-lifetime occasion," the woman continued.

"How much does it cost?" Mom challenged.

"Well, it is one of our more expensive dresses," the saleswoman admitted. "But it's a wonderful buy at $789."

Mom gulped. "Oh, my. We can't afford that," she said.

I was shocked, too. Why, a person could buy a moped with that kind of money.

An embarrassed silence lasted until Cheryl said, "Well, Dad did promise to pay for my dress."

"He'll never pay that much," Mom snorted. "You'll have to talk to him again before you can make any decisions."

"All right, I will," said my sister, turning to

admire herself from yet another angle.

"Maybe we should look at some less expensive dresses while we're here," Mom suggested.

Cheryl shook her head stubbornly. "I don't want to look at any other wedding dresses, but I would like to see some bridesmaid's gowns," she said.

"What color?" asked the saleswoman, smiling again.

"Blue, pink or burgundy," said Cheryl. "Something that would look good on my sister." She smiled at me.

"About a size six, I would say," the woman decided, and she disappeared. A little shiver of excitement ran through me. Was there a chance that a mere dress could work miracles on me the way it had for Cheryl? I wondered.

The first dress I tried on certainly didn't do it. The front was way too big for me, and it hung in a limp mass of ruffles. The second one was just as bad except it included a little cape to cover me up. But the third dress was the answer to my prayers. It had a high collar, long see-through sleeves, and trim lines that made me look sophisticated rather than bony. My skin seemed to glow in the dress' particular shade of blue, and its soft filmy fabric made me feel good all over. I turned around and around in front of the mirror wondering if what I saw could really be me.

"That dress looks super on you," Cheryl bubbled. "That's it. That's the one we'll use."

Mom checked the price tag, and she nodded. "I think it's a good choice," she agreed.

Cheryl added, "Since I want you to be my maid of honor you'll wear blue. The other bridesmaids will wear the same dress in pink. Everyone should look really nice."

"You mean I get to wear this dress as your maid of honor?" I asked eagerly. Suddenly the whole idea of a wedding was a lot more attractive to me.

Seven

BEFORE we left the bridal department of the store, the saleswoman warned us that we must allow two-to-three months for delivery on the dresses. The minute we got home Cheryl hurried into the kitchen to call Dad, shutting the door firmly behind her. When she came charging out of the kitchen a few minutes later, we sort of guessed what he'd said. Cheryl ran straight for her room bawling her eyes out.

During the next few weeks Mom and Cheryl talked endlessly about the wedding. Rachel and Mrs. Block called with all sorts of suggestions of where to have it. Still nothing had been decided. At last Cheryl agreed to hold the ceremony in our church after all. She finally realized that marching around someone's backyard to the strains of a portable organ really couldn't compare with coming down the aisle in a candlelit church.

When she mentioned her plans to our minister, however, he told her that every weekend in June and most of those in May were already spoken for. Several Saturdays even had double headers scheduled. She could either take May eighteenth or wait until July. Mom and I pushed hard for July, but Cheryl decided on May eighteenth.

"But you won't even be done with final exams then," Mom pointed out.

"I don't care," my sister said stubbornly. "Matthew will be leaving in June, and I'm going with him."

Mom and I just looked at each other and shook our heads. Cheryl could really be impossible sometimes.

The following Saturday Cheryl said, "I'd better order the invitations tomorrow."

"We'll need a place for the reception before you can do that," Mom said. So right after lunch Cheryl started calling around town to find a place. When I got back from Heidi's three hours later, she was still at it.

"If only the church wasn't having a bazaar that afternoon," Cheryl complained.

"May certainly is a busy month," Mom sighed.

"Maybe you could have the reception here," I suggested.

"Here?" my sister said scornfully. "There wouldn't be enough room."

Mom, however, looked thoughtful. "You were thinking about a garden ceremony. Why not have a backyard reception?" she pointed out. "We could clean up the garage and use it in case of rain."

"The garage?" Cheryl protested. "Mom, that's tacky."

"It doesn't have to be with the right decorations," Mom said.

"But Mom, I want my reception to be impressive," Cheryl wailed.

Mom rolled her eyes. "Then you'd better talk to your father," she snapped.

"Good idea," Cheryl said quickly. "Can I use the phone in your bedroom?"

Mom shrugged and Cheryl disappeared. A little while later she returned with a big smile on her face. She announced, "Rachel said we can have the reception at their place. She even offered to take care of all the details. Isn't that great?"

"Just peachy," Mom said sarcastically. "I think I'll stay home."

"Aw Mom, don't be like that," Cheryl pleaded. "They have a great big fancy place that's just perfect for something like this."

"I know," answered Mom. "They have a beautiful home and plenty of money to throw around while I've had to struggle to raise my five

51

children." Mom wasn't very happy about that.

"Well, maybe that's why Dad and Rachel are so eager to help now," Cheryl reasoned. "I think this offer is pretty nice of them."

Mom made a deep sigh. "I wish I could see it that way. Well, at least I'll have one less thing to worry about," she added.

Now that Cheryl had a time and a place for her extravaganza, she began to look through wedding announcements and invitations that she'd saved from some of her friends' weddings. Before long I saw that she was crying. I couldn't figure out why.

"What's the matter?" I asked, coming over to her.

She sobbed noisily. "None of these will work for me," she managed.

I looked at the elegant folders in front of her. "Why not?" I asked.

"Just read one, and you'll see," she sniffed.

I read: "Mr. and Mrs. J. Michael Lerner request the honor of your presence at the marriage of their daughter, Denise, to Mr. William E. Smith, son of Dr. and Mrs. Jason W. Smith . . ." and I was still mystified. "What's the matter with that?" I wanted to know.

"Don't you see?" she wailed. "Mom and Dad aren't Mr. and Mrs. Anybody anymore."

"Oh, yeah," I realized.

"And Mr. Norman Wood and Mrs. Roger Murphy sounds terrible," she cried.

Cheryl had a point, so I leafed through the other invitations to see what I could suggest. "Hey, here's one where only the mother did the inviting," I said, handing it to her.

She grabbed it and read eagerly: "Mrs. Grace Butler White requests the honor . . ." Then she started to cry again.

"Now what's the matter?" I insisted.

"Penny Butler's dad is dead," she said. "My dad is not only alive, but he's paying for the whole thing."

"Oh," I said. "I guess you can't use that." Then I had an idea. "Try not to worry about it," I said. "Lots of people are divorced these days. I'll bet the place that sells invitations will know the right way to handle this."

She stopped crying and considered my words. Then drying her eyes, she said, "You're right, of course. Thanks, Roxie."

"Don't mention it," I said, looking at the invitations spread before us. Then I had another thought. "Say Cheryl, did you ever think about what your full name will be after the wedding?" I asked.

She gave me a puzzled look. "No, why?" she asked.

"Oh, no reason. I just think Cheryl Wood

Block sounds sort of funny. That's all," I grinned, trying not to laugh.

That made Cheryl start to cry harder than ever. "You think this whole wedding is funny," she blubbered. "None of you want me to get married, and you all are just awful. Go away and leave me alone." I knew I should have quit while I was ahead.

In spite of everything, the wedding did start to take shape over the next few days. Cheryl finally found a cheaper wedding dress that she liked, the printers had a very suitable wording for her invitations, and we managed to convince Matt's mother that we couldn't have country-western music at the ceremony. We were even getting used to our daily call from Rachel.

When the phone rang late one night, I automatically said, "Yes, Cheryl's in the living room. I'll get her."

Still clutching several pages of her term paper, Cheryl picked up the phone, and continued reading as she listened. Then her face began to cloud up and she sputtered, "Well no, Tanya, I didn't do it on purpose. Yes, I'm sure you're upset, but . . . Well most of the dresses are already ordered. I don't know what we're going to do. Can I call you back a little later? I'm pretty busy right now . . . Yes, yes, I will . . . Bye."

"Who was that?" I asked anxiously. "And

what's the matter with the dresses?"

"That was Matthew's sister," Cheryl explained. "We have a problem. She hates her dress and she's throwing a fit about it."

"But what's wrong? The dresses are beautiful," I insisted.

"Tanya is a redhead," Cheryl groaned. "And she absolutely refuses to wear pink."

"That's too bad," I said angrily. "I'm glad I'm wearing blue because mine is already ordered."

But Cheryl wasn't listening to me now. She was on the way out of the kitchen yelling, "Mom, Mom . . ."

Eight

"MOM, what are we going to do?" cried Cheryl. "All the wedding stuff has been planned in blue and pink. We can't change everything just because of one bridesmaid."

"Let's kick Matt's sister out of the wedding," I suggested.

"Good idea," Cheryl said fiercely.

Mom frowned. "Now girls, you know that won't work," she said.

I tried again. "Make her dye her hair?" I suggested.

"Roxie," Mom ordered. "Don't be ridiculous."

"Well, what are we going to do?" Cheryl wanted to know.

Mom sighed. "That's a good question," she said wearily. "How about having all of your bridesmaids in blue or in a rainbow effect, you know, one of each color."

"With seven bridesmaids?" Cheryl snorted. "I'm not sure there are that many colors. Besides, several of the dresses are already ordered. We can't back out now."

"Then how about alternating blue and pink?" Mom suggested.

"I've never seen that done before," Cheryl protested.

Mom shrugged. "Neither have I, but I don't think it would look too bad," she said.

"Maybe not," sniffed Cheryl, "but I wanted my wedding to be perfect. Instead we have one problem after the other."

Mom patted her on the shoulder. "If this is the worst crisis we face, we'll be very lucky," she said, gently.

The invitations came the next day, and we set to work on them that very night. By bedtime we must have addressed a million, but there were plenty more left. I had a track meet the following evening, and I was hoping the invitations would be finished by the time I got home. But I had no such luck. Mom and Cheryl were still writing steadily and Brenda was licking stamps.

Mom stopped when she saw me. "How did you do at the meet?" she asked.

"Really good," I bragged. "I won the hurdles and got a third in the long jump."

"Congratulations," they all said.

"I left some stew on the stove for you," Mom continued. "You can help us with the invitations once you're finished eating."

58

"Okay," I agreed and got myself a plate of food.

"This list seems incredibly long," Mom told Cheryl. "How many people are we inviting anyway?"

"We're up to about 350 now," Cheryl said. "I guess the Blocks know everyone in town."

"Let's hope they can't all come," I said.

"I'm tired of licking stamps," Brenda complained. "My tongue feels all fuzzy."

"Why don't you get ready for bed?" Mom asked. "Roxie's here to take over." Brenda quickly disappeared.

I finished my stew and sat down. Mom was looking at the list again. "By the way," she told Cheryl. "We need to add great-aunt Florence and her family to the list. They live in Los Angeles, and we haven't seen them in years. But cousin Mildred thought Florence would be insulted if we didn't send her an invitation."

Cheryl drew a deep breath. "How many of them are there?" she asked.

"Let me see," said Mom, getting herself a cup of coffee. "Florence has three daughters. Betty Jo has two kids, Marcy has five, and Delia has three. That makes a total of seventeen."

I just shook my head. A few more people and we'd have to have two performances of this wedding.

We had another track meet on Saturday, and again I won the hurdles. I did it in really good time, too. "You looked fantastic today," Heidi told me as we walked home. "Why, you're a cinch to win the conference title this year."

"Thanks, I hope you're right," I said, trying to sound humble.

Just then Heidi asked, "Hey, what's happening at your house?"

I looked ahead to see my whole family streaming out the front door carrying boxes. "I don't know," I said stupidly. "Maybe we've had a bomb threat or something." I caught up with Brenda and asked, "Hey, shrimp, what gives?"

She turned just long enough to say, "Somebody named Florence is coming, and Mom seems awfully scared of her."

Heidi and I looked at each other and shrugged. I ought to know better than to ask a five-year-old anything.

Roger was returning to the house just then, so I asked him next. "What's going on?"

He gave me a dismal look and said, "Your mother has decided to clean the basement, and I'm missing the basketball game on T.V." With that he stalked off.

"Weddings," growled Jeremy as he passed. "There ought to be a law against them."

Cheryl and Jason were behind him. "Why

didn't you just elope?" Jason griped to his sister.

A voice from somewhere below us said, "Roxie, don't just stand there. Get down here and help me with this old chair." Heidi said it was time for her to go home. She left in a hurry.

Although cleaning the basement was hard work, we sure found some neat stuff. Of course Mom wanted to throw most of it away, but we wouldn't let her. "Gee, I forgot we had this," said Cheryl, fingering an old croquet mallet.

"Hey, let me see," cried Jeremy, grabbing it from her. "I used to be pretty good at this."

"Remember how silly Dad used to get when he played?" Jason asked softly.

"Will you guys teach me how to play sometime?" Brenda wanted to know.

"Get a load of this old hat," giggled Jeremy as he plopped a calico bonnet on Cheryl's head.

"Howdy there, school marm. How about a little kiss?" Jason teased, putting his arm around her.

Roger struck a John Wayne pose and boomed, "Unhand that woman, ya lily-livered snake." Everyone laughed.

"Here's something we can throw away," I said. "We surely don't need this old moth-eaten bird."

Jason quickly snatched the stuffed monstrosity from me. "Don't throw that away," he protested hotly. "I won that at a Cub Scout jamboree."

By the end of the day we were all exhausted, but we were also happy. Jeremy gave up his tape and earphones to play cards with Jason and Brenda. Mom and Roger retired to the den to discuss the kitchen remodeling. Cheryl and I lay on the living room rug looking at wedding cake pictures.

"You're not going to have a little bride and groom on the top, are you?" I asked hopefully.

"No, those dolls are always ugly," she said. "I thought I'd have bells instead."

"You know, today was really kind of fun," I said. "I've never seen Roger fit in so well around here."

"He's not a bad guy, really," Cheryl agreed.

"And the boys were a lot of help," I continued. "Just think, when you clean your basement, you won't have anyone to help but Matt."

"We'll only be able to afford a small apartment," she said soberly. "I don't think there'll be any basement to worry about for quite a while."

I looked away from her. "It's going to be weird around here without you," I mumbled.

"It's going to be weird for me, too," she admitted as she put her arm around me.

"I'll bet you'll be lonesome," I added.

"Maybe I will at first," she said.

"Then why don't you just forget the whole thing and stay here?" I asked desperately.

She gave a little laugh that was almost like a sob and said, "I can't do that now."

"Why not?" I demanded. "It would save everyone a lot of trouble."

Before she could answer Jeremy yelled, "Roxie, telephone," and I had to go.

"Roxie," said Heidi's voice, "I was just reading the paper, and it had a story about the All-Conference track meet. Guess when they're having it?"

She sounded all excited, and I wondered what was up. "When?" I asked nervously.

"May eighteenth," she pronounced very carefully.

"Oh, my gosh," I groaned. "How can I get out of Cheryl's wedding?"

Nine

"YOU can't just skip your sister's wedding," Heidi protested.

"But she shouldn't be getting married in the first place," I said bitterly. "It'll never work."

"That's just your opinion," Heidi pointed out. "And you are the maid of honor so you'll have to be there."

I knew she was right. If Cheryl is going to get married, I'll have to be there even if I'm dying of typhoid. "Aw heck," I bellowed, giving the nearest chair a kick. "I don't suppose I could talk her into postponing it."

"Not with the invitations already sent," Heidi said.

"Well, maybe I could run the hurdles and still make it to the wedding," I said.

Heidi snorted. "I really doubt it. The meet is clear over in Mitchell."

I scratched my head and squirmed. "What if Cheryl catches the chicken pox? I could find some little kid to give her the germs," I said.

"Roxie!" Heidi cried in a shocked voice. "That's a terrible idea."

"Yeah, it is," I realized. "She's already had chicken pox anyway. But I have to be at that track meet. Maybe Jason and Jeremy could help me sabotage Cheryl's plans."

Heidi groaned. "Why don't you just forget about the track meet and enjoy the wedding? You do want to wear that blue dress, don't you?"

"Not as much as I want to win the hurdles..." I began.

"Sorry, I can't talk anymore," Heidi cut in. "Dad wants to use the phone."

I hung up and peeked through the door at Cheryl. She was still engrossed in her cake book, unaware of how I was plotting against her. I quietly walked past her and joined Jason and Jeremy in the family room. Brenda was on her way to bed. The boys had started to play chess, and neither of them looked up as I dropped into the bean bag in the corner. I sat quietly as I considered what approach to use on the boys. A pitch for family unity might be more effective than the truth about my track meet, I decided.

"Hi, who's winning?" I asked brightly.

"Who invited you?" grumbled Jason. He's always grumpy when he's losing.

"Nobody invited me," I admitted. "But this is

the family room, and I'm part of the family."

"Humph," said Jason.

I hummed a few nervous little notes at that and squirmed.

"Shhh," ordered Jason.

I squirmed silently from then on. Finally I said, "We sure have a nice family, don't we?"

Jason snapped, "It's just fine except for you. Get lost."

"Well, excuuuse me," I shouted and stomped out slamming the door. The boys certainly weren't going to be any help.

Cheryl looked up as I shuffled by her. "What was all that about?" she asked.

"Nothing," I muttered. "Guess I'll go up to my room now. Good night."

I racked my brain for a plan all that night and all the next day. Then something Cheryl said at supper gave me hope. "Today Matt told me his sisters are complaining about the hats they're supposed to wear," she said, crossing her eyes. "Sometimes I think I'll just cancel the whole affair if one more problem comes up."

That's it, I thought to myself. I just have to make sure Cheryl has a few more little problems.

My first chance to make trouble came after school on Monday. Cheryl announced she was going to the florist. I quickly convinced her that I should go along. Brenda wanted to go, too, so we set off together.

A plump woman at the florist gave us pictures to look at and lots of free advice. "Roses are always good," she said cheerfully. "Or these daisies would be nice for a spring wedding."

"I like those," Brenda decided. "They look like dandelions."

"I don't know what I'm going to do," Cheryl said with a sigh. "Half of my bridesmaids will be in blue and the rest in pink. Do you have any blue flowers?"

The woman nodded eagerly. "We could dye some white carnations blue or just dip their edges if you prefer," she said.

Cheryl looked thoughtful. "May I see some of them?" she asked.

The woman agreed and disappeared in the back room. As soon as she returned with the flowers I began to sneeze noisily.

"Bless you," said the florist. "Many people are allergic to carnations, so let's try something else."

She tried again and again with many types of flowers, but each time I sneezed madly. By now the woman was frowning and Cheryl was getting upset. "This is all I need," she kept muttering.

Finally the woman brought an especially pretty bouquet of daisies and pushed them right under my nose. "How about these?" she

68

challenged. When I sneezed again, she looked at me suspiciously and said, "That's odd."

"I don't see why," Cheryl grumbled. "My sister seems to be allergic to every other flower in the world. Why not these?"

"Because these are silk flowers," the woman announced. My sneezing was immediately cured.

"Fake flowers," said Brenda. "They don't even smell."

Cheryl was angry. "Fake flowers and fake sneezes," she fumed. "Roxie, go wait in the car."

When she finally came out, Cheryl checked Brenda's seat belt roughly and fiercely gunned the motor. Without looking at me, she said, "That was absolutely disgusting. Wait until I tell Mom."

I gulped and thought about what Mom would say. Yup, I was in big trouble.

But when we got home Mom was in too big a tizzy to do more than threaten to ground me for life if I didn't shape up. You see, Rachel was on her way over to discuss reception plans with Cheryl. Since Rachel had never been to our house before, Mom was determined to make it look its best. She dusted frantically and kept us hopping with orders like, "Pick up those socks and put them in the hamper." By the time the door bell rang the house looked okay, but we were all winded. Cheryl smoothed her hair and hurried to the door while Mom disappeared into the kitchen.

"Hello, Rachel, it's awfully nice of you to come by," my sister said warmly.

Rachel, standing there in a trim gray suit, smiled and said, "Well, I know how busy you are these days." Then, as she started through the door, she added, "I hope you won't mind that I brought the boys along."

"Oh, no," I said to myself. "We just love having spoiled brats around." Where could I hide?

Cheryl showed Rachel and the boys into the living room. Then Cheryl and Rachel began to talk about refreshments. After a few minutes of sizing up the situation, the smaller boy began to switch the lamp on and off. Thor got down on the floor and began retrieving dust from under the couch.

I knew Mom wouldn't approve of that so I said, "Brenda, why don't you take the boys outside and find something for them to do?"

Brenda twisted her fingers in a long golden curl and shook her head shyly, but Rachel picked up on my suggestion. "Why Brenda, you and the boys could have a fine time," she coaxed. "Maybe you could show them your room."

"Oh, no, that was my room, too," I said to

myself. I was glad Brenda didn't think much of the idea. Unfortunately, Cheryl decided it was time to take charge. "Brenda, please take the boys upstairs," she ordered.

Brenda made a face and moved slowly toward the stairs with the boys curiously following. I would have followed them right then if Mom hadn't stuck her head out of the kitchen to ask me to help serve coffee. Why does everyone that comes over have to have coffee? I wondered.

When I finally carried in a tray of coffee and cookies, I started up the stairs to see what the boys were doing to my room. I hadn't gone very far when the stampede hit. First, something furry ran between my feet, and then the boys bowled over me. I landed with a thud and would have lain there a minute if it hadn't been for the screaming. Then I saw Brenda, and I thought she'd been scalped!

Ten

"**WAIT!** Stop!" I yelled after the running boys. They didn't stop and Brenda was still screaming. About that time Mom charged into the living room to save Brenda, and Cheryl and Rachel each managed to grab a boy. I found the gerbil.

Mom looked hard at Brenda and gasped, "What have those animals done to you?"

I thought that was perfectly obvious. They'd cut off all her hair.

"Thor, Obediah," Rachel said sternly to her sons. "This was most uncalled for. Running through Mrs. Murphy's house is simply not acceptable."

"That's not all they did," I pointed out, but Rachel didn't answer.

Finally Brenda stopped crying long enough to explain that the boys had been fascinated with the way her doll's hair changed lengths by way of a knob. I guess that's what gave them the idea to give each other cuts. When the boys decided

Homer needed one too, however, Brenda panicked. In the struggle, the gerbil escaped and my sister had been trying to catch her pet in order to protect him.

"There, there, baby," Mom told Brenda. "We won't let those awful boys bother you and Homer anymore."

Rachel looked a little miffed about that. "Well, I'm sure the boys are sorry about her hair," she said evenly. "But you know how children are."

"They ought to be sorry," Cheryl fired back. "I don't see how Brenda can even be in the wedding now."

"Oh, nonsense," Rachel scoffed. "It isn't that bad, and her hair will grow back."

"Not in time for the wedding," Mom said angrily. "Those boys should be punished severely for this."

"I'll thank you not to tell me how to raise my children," said Rachel.

"Someone needs to," snapped Mom.

Rachel's nostrils flared. "Well!" she huffed. "I've never been so insulted in my life, and Cheryl, you can forget about any further help from me or your father." And with that she gathered up her sons and stormed out of the house.

As soon as the door slammed, Brenda buried her face on Mom's shoulder and began to howl.

This time Mom and Cheryl joined her.

About that time Roger came through the door wearing a smile that quickly fell. "What's the matter?" he asked in a hushed tone. When they didn't answer, he asked, "Has something happened to Jason or Jeremy?"

Mom shook her head and managed, "No, it's that awful woman Norman married. She was just here, and her two little boys attacked Brenda."

Roger stared at Brenda. Smoke started pouring out of his ears and I could tell he was getting the wrong idea. So I said, "It wasn't really an attack. They were just playing."

He took Brenda's face in both his hands and insisted, "Brenda, tell me why you're crying."

She sniffed and snuffed and finally whined, "Cheryl says I can't be her flower girl now."

"Well, I'm sure she didn't mean that," he said soothingly. "You're going to be a beautiful flower girl even if I have to buy you a wig."

That got Brenda's attention. "Can I have a ponytail like my Tracy doll?" she asked.

Roger shrugged and nodded. Then, turning to Cheryl he pleaded, "Now what's the matter with you?"

She blew her nose and blubbered, "Rachel was supposed to take care of the reception. Now she's mad, and she said Dad won't help either."

That ought to stop the wedding, I thought

gleefully. But Roger had to say, "I'm sure we can still straighten things out with your father, and we'll just have the reception here."

When Mom realized what he'd said, she started crying harder. At that Roger threw up his hands and left. All-Conference track meet, here I come, I thought happily.

Supper that night was very late and everyone was crabby. We hadn't quite finished when the door bell rang. Brenda went to answer it and returned with Matt who looked terrific in shorts and a T-shirt.

"What are you doing here?" Cheryl asked sullenly.

He looked a little surprised. "Oh, I didn't know you were eating," he explained. "I just thought you might want to play some tennis."

"Tennis?" she exploded. "Is that all you have to think about?" she asked. "I'm facing a major disaster here, and you want to play tennis?"

"What's wrong?" he asked, dropping into the chair next to her.

"Everything," she wailed. "For starters, Rachel's mad at us, and our reception is off."

"Gosh, that's too bad," he said thoughtfully. "I wonder if my mom would take over and have the thing at our house."

Cheryl stopped sniffling and looking forlorn. "Matthew! Do you think she would?" she asked.

"You have to call her about it right away!"

"Well, I can't do that," he told her. "Mom and Dad are out of town, but I'll ask her as soon as they get back."

Cheryl jumped to her feet then and hugged him hard. "Oh, I'm sure you'll talk her into it, and I feel so much better."

"Then let's play tennis," he said, grinning.

She frowned. "No, I'm sorry. I have a paper due in child development."

He looked disappointed. "Gee, I'll be glad when school and this wedding are over," he complained.

*   *   *   *   *

I had a super run at the hurdles the next afternoon. My strides were paced just perfect for each fence and my time was blazingly fast. "That's the way, Roxie," Coach Edmunds had said proudly. "If you do that well at the championships, you'll win for sure."

After practice the coach handed out permission slips for the bus that would take us to Mitchell. We were to bring them back to school with our parents' signatures. "Why did you take one of those slips?" Heidi asked as we headed home. "You have a wedding to go to that day."

"There's not going to be a wedding," I insisted.

"Who says?" Heidi asked.

"Well, Cheryl's just about changed her mind several times," I said.

"Roxie," Heidi said firmly, "there *is* going to be a wedding, and you've got to tell the coach about it."

"There's still time for it to be cancelled," I said through clenched teeth.

* * * * *

The next night Heidi and I were at my house watching T.V. when the phone rang. The private eye we were watching was in a real tight spot so I didn't answer it at first. When the phone kept ringing and ringing, I got to my feet.

"Hello, is this the Roger Murphy residence?" asked a voice I didn't recognize.

"Yes," I said.

"Well, this is Florence Dickerson, and I'm at the airport. Why hasn't anyone come to meet me?" she asked.

"Just a minute," I said. "Mom," I screamed, "it's for you!"

"Who is it?" she called back.

"A Florence Dickerson," I said.

Mom hurried through the kitchen door

muttering, "Oh, my goodness. Florence is calling from Boston."

"She isn't calling from Boston," I said. "Florence is at the airport!"

"Good heavens, give me that," gasped Mom, grabbing the phone out of my hands. "Hello, Florence, where are you? . . . But I thought your card said the seventeenth . . . The seventh? Oh, yes, we'll be down to pick you up right away."

She dropped the phone in its cradle and looked around wildly. "Where's Roger?" Mom asked. "He can go to the airport while I get a room ready for Florence."

"He's at a meeting. He said he wouldn't be back until around ten o'clock," I reminded her.

"Oh, dear, then I'll have to go myself. Roxie, you'll have to change the sheets on Cheryl's bed and straighten up. Then make one of the boy's beds for Cheryl and fix the cots in the basement for Jason and Jeremy."

"Awe, Mom . . . " I began. But she just gave me one of her LOOKS and vanished into the night.

"Thanks a lot, Florence," I said to the closing door. "I'll bet she's a fat old blabbermouth," I said to myself.

Eleven

MY guess about Florence turned out to be way off. She was pretty old, but she had a terrific figure and she didn't waste words. She even insisted on carrying her own bags upstairs before she joined us in the living room.

Mom tried to make small talk. "Well, it certainly is nice that you could come for Cheryl's wedding," she said with a smile. "How was your flight?"

"Very ordinary," said Florence.

"How are your daughters and their families?" Mom asked.

"Betty Jo filed for divorce last week," Florence said.

Mom sputtered, "What a shame. How long have they been married?"

"Fifteen years. It came as quite a shock to all of us," Florence added.

"I'm sure it did," Mom responded. "Divorce is so unpleasant, especially with children involved."

About that time I decided to go to bed early. I

didn't need anyone to tell me about divorce.

I set my alarm for 6 A.M. and the next morning I thought I was the only one up. But the bathroom door was already locked when I got there. I heard splashing and singing coming from inside, and I knew it had to be Florence. Nobody in my family sings in the tub and certainly not early in the morning.

Suddenly the door opened to reveal a figure in pink lace wearing a mask of mud. Florence caught her breath when she saw me. "Oh, I didn't know anyone else was awake," she explained.

"I didn't either," I told her. "I often run before school."

"You say you're going out to run?" she asked eagerly. "I always run before breakfast at home. Would you mind if I came along?"

What could I say? You're an old woman. You'd slow me down? "Not at all," I agreed. "I'll meet you out front."

I figured she'd keep me waiting while she got beautiful, but by the time I'd gotten into my running clothes, Florence was already outside. She wore a black jogging suit that said "Boston Bombers" on the back and a matching headband. She looked as if she meant business.

We started coasting down Maple Street, each guessing how fast the other might want to go. Gradually we picked up speed, and by the time we hit Cleveland Avenue we were moving. I was beginning to worry that I'd be the one left behind when she slowed to a walk.

"I suppose you have to get back pretty soon for school," she said, barely panting. I nodded breathlessly, and we turned around.

"Are you in training for something special or do you just like to run?" she asked.

"I'm on the track team at school," I said.

"Oh, really? What's your event?" she asked. She sounded really interested.

"The hurdles," I answered, looking at her shyly. "I have a good shot at the All-Conference title, too."

Her smile was enthusiastic. "That's wonderful. When are the championships? I'd certainly like to be there," she said.

"Weekend after next," I said automatically.

"Why, that's the same weekend as Cheryl's wedding," she realized. "Can you manage both?"

"I'm not sure," I admitted. Why did she have to bring that up?

We walked on silently for a while when, out of the blue, she asked, "Do you think Cheryl's ready for marriage?"

Wow! I couldn't believe she was asking *me* that. I certainly didn't know what to say. "Well, she's kind of flighty," I hedged. "Somehow I just can't picture her as a happy homemaker."

Florence grinned and nodded. "I met your sister last night after you went to bed, and I know what you mean," she said.

We walked some more as my mind raced. Florence was an adult, and she didn't think Cheryl should get married either. Would she help me stop the wedding? I wondered.

"What do you think of Cheryl's fiancé?" was her next question.

"He's gorgeous," I responded without thinking. "I mean, he's very good looking and nice and all, but I don't think he's quite ready for marriage either."

"What makes you say that?" Florence asked.

"Oh, nothing special. It's just a feeling I have," I said.

"Hmmm," said Florence.

* * * * *

I'd only been home from school a few minutes that night when Matt arrived looking for Cheryl. "The girls are giving her a bridal shower this afternoon," I told him. "She should be home pretty soon."

He shrugged and turned to go. "Oh, well, I'll give her a call later."

But Florence appeared just then. "Hello,

there," she said warmly. "You must be Matthew. I'm Cheryl's great-aunt Florence, and I've been dying to meet you."

"Oh, hi," he answered, taking the hand she offered.

"Your big day is just around the corner. Are you getting excited?" she asked.

"Uh, sure," he said, nodding vaguely. "That's what I wanted to talk about with Cheryl. Mom says we can have the reception at our house."

"At your house? Is this a change in plans?" Florence asked.

"Uh, yeah. Cheryl had some kind of falling-out with her dad's new wife, and things are kind of confused," Matt said.

"Nothing serious, I hope," Florence probed.

"We don't know," he admitted. "She's been trying to get in touch with her dad for several days now, but he's never home."

"Have you found a place to live after the wedding?" Florence wanted to know.

"No, not yet. It's hard to find something I can afford," he said.

Florence nodded. "Yes, I understand you'll be going to graduate school."

"Oh, I have a job, too," he said quickly. "I'll be assisting the coaches."

"Goodness. You're going to be busy," Florence added.

"Yup," he agreed. "Say, it's been nice meeting you, but I have to run. Tell Cheryl I'll call her."

* * * * *

The next day Coach Edmunds asked me where my permission slip was, and I said I'd forgotten it. "She's going to be mad when you finally tell her the truth," Heidi warned.

Practice was extra-long that night, and when I did get home, there was a strange car in the driveway. I walked into the living room to find a woman with pinkish-red hair sitting on the sofa with Cheryl.

"Now I think a barbecue is the best way to handle a crowd," the woman was saying.

Cheryl looked doubtful. "A barbecue?" she muttered.

This must be Matt's mother, I thought to myself.

Twelve

MATT appeared a moment later with a glass of milk and a plate of cookies. "What do you think?" Cheryl asked him.

He swallowed a mouthful. "About what?" he mumbled.

"Your mom wants our reception to be a barbecue," she said.

"Sounds okay," he said, easing himself onto the floor.

"But we'll all be in long dresses and tuxedos. Don't you think a barbecue would be too messy?" Cheryl asked.

"It doesn't have to be," said Mrs. Block.

"And we sure aren't going to stay in those fancy clothes very long," Matt added. "I told my friends to bring their swimming suits."

Cheryl turned to face him. "Matthew, this isn't just any old party," she emphasized. "This is our wedding." He shrugged and took another cookie.

Just then the front door opened and Florence walked in followed by my father! I don't know who was more shocked, Cheryl or me.

"Dad, what are you doing here?" she gasped. "Why, I've been trying to call you."

"I've been working late and thinking a lot," he responded.

Then Florence introduced herself to Mrs. Block and Dad did the same. "It seems as if I've come at a bad time," he observed.

"Oh, no," Cheryl told him. "We were just making some plans for the wedding reception."

He nodded sheepishly. "I heard what happened with Rachel and the boys," he said. "All I can say is that I'm sorry about Brenda's hair."

Cheryl sniffed. "It wasn't your fault," she muttered. He started to say something then, but changed his mind.

"Well, what have the three of you been deciding?" Florence asked.

"Nothing really," Cheryl admitted. "Matt seems to think this should be a fun party, and I see it as a dress-up affair."

Dad took a step forward then, and I could see he was thinking hard. "That's what bothers me," he began. He cleared his throat as everybody looked at him. "I doubt if either one of you see this wedding for what it really is. Your wedding will actually be the start of a long, hard struggle."

Cheryl frowned, but Matt spoke up. "That

sounds pretty negative, Mr. Wood. I know it will be a little rough for the next few years since I'll be in grad school. But when I finally do come home at night, Cheryl will be waiting for me."

"That does sound nice," Dad agreed, " . . . for you. But what is Cheryl going to do besides wait? She has a brain and a future, too, you know."

Cheryl looked lovingly at Matt. "I have lots of time to do what I want after Matthew is finished with grad school," she assured us. "Right now I'm going to get a job and help pay his way."

"That wouldn't be necessary if Dad wasn't so cheap," Matt said bitterly.

"Your father is not cheap," Mrs. Block objected. "It's just that he fails to see why you should run off to grad school when there's a perfectly good job waiting for you at Destinkly Yours."

"But I'm not ready to settle down to a job like that yet," Matt shot back. "I need to try a few other things before I'm tied down for life."

Cheryl looked surprised. "Why, I thought you were going to get your master's degree because you knew what you wanted to do," she said. "What if you change your mind about being a coach? What if you change your mind about being married?"

For several minutes no one spoke. It was so quiet I was almost embarrassed to breathe.

Finally, Dad broke the silence. "I'm not sure how to put this," he said with difficulty. "I only know that marriage can be the worst pain in the world if you're tied to the wrong person, and divorce just gives you a new set of problems."

It seemed to me that Cheryl and Matt were really listening at last. Mrs. Block must have thought so too because she said, "Maybe you both need time to figure out who you are. There's still time to cancel the wedding."

"Cancel the wedding?" Cheryl protested. "After all the time we've spent planning it?"

Matt looked shocked. "Our friends are all looking forward to it," he said.

Then Cheryl's mouth opened, but she didn't say anything. Instead she turned to stare at Matt until he returned her gaze. "Maybe we need to talk about this," she said at last. "Come on in the kitchen."

When they had gone the rest of us sort of smiled at each other uncomfortably. "Well, do you think they'll . . . " Mrs. Block began.

But just then we heard loud voices from outside, and one of them sounded like Mom's. "I don't care about your contract," she cried angrily. "You can't come this week."

The door burst open and Mom charged in yelling, "Roger, Roger, are you home yet?" She stopped in her tracks when she saw the rest of us.

Red with embarrassment, she added, "Oh, I didn't know we had company."

"Hello, Grace," said my father.

"Mrs. Block, this is Cheryl's mother," Florence said.

"You'll have to excuse me," Mom sputtered. "I don't usually come into the house like that. It's just that I'm so upset."

"What's going on out there?" I wanted to know.

That got Mom all steamed up again. "The contractor for the kitchen got here about the same time I did," she explained. "He insists that our contract says they can start work at their earliest convenience, and he wants to start tearing the place apart tomorrow."

"But the wedding is only a few days away," Mrs. Block realized.

"Exactly," said Mom. "And I can only handle one big deal at a time."

I hadn't heard Cheryl and Matt return, but suddenly Cheryl's voice said, "What if there wasn't going to be any other 'big deal' next week?" Mom spun around in surprise as Cheryl continued. "What if we had the wedding a little later, say next year?"

"Yeah," Matt added eagerly. "We wouldn't want to stop your kitchen from getting remodeled."

Mom's mouth dropped open. "Huh? You mean you'd postpone your wedding over something like this?" she asked.

"Well, that's not the only reason," Cheryl admitted.

Then a strange thing happened. You would have thought someone would have been upset. All those songs on the radio say that a broken engagement is something to cry about. But instead, we all broke into huge grins. Mom was so happy she grabbed Cheryl in a great big hug, and Mrs. Block threw her arms around Matt. Florence patted Cheryl on the back and winked at me.

Dad was just standing by himself looking sort of out of place so I walked over to him. "Dad," I said, putting my hand on his arm. "Dad, thanks. You came through after all."

He shrugged and looked at the floor. "I'm glad you feel that way," he said softly, "because I've messed up a lot of things I've done lately."

I couldn't stand to see him looking unhappy so I gave him a hug. He really looked at me then, and sort of pushed me toward the door. "Roxie, I need to talk to you," he insisted.

Neither of us said anything as he led me over to the old porch swing. We sat down together. He just kept looking at me until he finally shook his head. "I want you to know that I'd give everything I own to have you kids back with me again," he said. He hesitated before going on quickly. "That day Rachel came over here with the boys, we had a terrible fight, and I moved out. She's a terrific person, but we just can't live together."

"Dad, that's awful," I sputtered. "What will you do now?"

He made sort of a face. "Well, I'm confused about a lot of things these days, but I've made one decision. I'm going to be a father again to you kids if it's not too late. Florence tells me you're a real track star, and I didn't even know about it."

I blushed at his words. "Oh, Dad, I'm not really a star," I protested. "But I am running in the All-Conference championships next weekend. Would you come?"

He beamed and gave me a big hug. "You bet I will," he said eagerly. "In fact, there's only one thing I'd like better."

I was mystified. "What's that?"

He grinned. "I want to see my little girl looking all grown up in the blue dress Cheryl told me about," he said, winking.

"Oh, Dad," I said shyly. "Do you really?"

"More than anything," he answered, ruffling my hair. "Florence predicts you're going to be a very pretty young lady, and I can see she's right."

*   *   *   *   *

You know, for a long time after Mom and Dad got divorced, I felt like a real nothing. Well, things are better now. I won the championship in the hurdles, my braces come off next month, and every once in a while someone actually listens to me at the supper table. Maybe it won't be so awful if Cheryl does get married next year, that is if my blue dress still fits.